Tell Me This Isn't Happening!

Collected by Robynn Clairday

P9-DGF-000

SCHOLASTIC INC.
New York Toronto London Auckland Sydney
Mexico City New Delhi Hong Kong

ISBN 0-439-09502-6

Copyright © 1999 by Robynn Clairday.
All rights reserved. Published by Scholastic Inc.
SCHOLASTIC and associated logos are trademarks and/or registered trademarks of Scholastic Inc.

12 11 10 9 8 7 6 5 4 3 2   9/9 0 1 2 3/0

Printed in the U.S.A.
First Scholastic printing, September 1999

Acknowledgments

I'd like to thank the many wonderful people who made this book possible.

First, my gratitude goes to Matt Clairday, who has always believed in me and who has always supported me, no matter what hardships had to be endured. You've made all of my dreams possible.

Also, a special thanks goes to my kind, generous, and very talented editor, Kate Egan.

I'd like to acknowledge Helene Reisler for going way beyond the call of duty and for being so enthusiastic about this project.

I'd also like to thank the following marvelous, big-hearted souls who worked hard and went to incredible lengths to help me get this book together: Suzanne Churchman, Andrew McBride, Jennifer Morales from CyberGrrlz, Sara from the Pony Show, David Davenport from The Young Writers Club, Michelle Churchman, Blythe Cameron from Tidbits, the Writers Page, Bob Reap from Teachers.Net, Kristin Bishop, Sean Davan, Elaine Bradley, Angela Goode, Bessie Clairday Manuel, Jessica Jiranek, Jennifer McCalley from Nickelodeon, Brian Bierley from the Detroit

Vipers, KeJuan Wilkins from the Detroit Lions, Debbie Johns from the Detroit Skating Club, Elite, *Essence* magazine, Laura Diaco, *Inscriptions*, Inkspot, Margie from the Novi Library, Wendy Bruetsch from Waldenbooks/Somerset Mall, Greg Yatst from Book Market, Glenda Cole, Bridget Mangiapane and Susan Nassar from Great Lakes Crossing Mall, Mrs. Williams from Walled Lake Library, Amy Irish from the Detroit Pistons, and all of those brilliant, erudite people who contributed to the Words of Wisdom sections.

I also can't forget the Bloomfield Township Library writers' group: Marilyn Spencer, Kari Cimbalik, Rowena Cherry, Tim Patrick, and Pat Washburn. You guys are the best!

Thank you, also, Margot and Sandy Reisler and Melyssa Cooke for providing endless encouragement and good wishes throughout all of my career. You are more than just family.

To Terry LaFin, forever a soul sister and an inspiration for this book.

And, of course, a giant thank-you to all of the incredible, funny, gifted kids who sent me their stories. I can't mention your names, but you know who you are.

Thank you, thank you, thank you!

Tell Me This Isn't Happening

It's gonna happen. To you, to me, to everyone you know. I promise. Before you know it — you'll be living that incredibly embarrassing moment when you wish with all your heart a spaceship would appear to lift you off the planet. . . .

Humiliation can hit at any time. Like, you could be sitting for an hour in class with blue ink all over your face and hands, not realizing that your pen had exploded. Yeah, a whole hour. This happened to me, as you may have already guessed.

Someone finally came over and said, "Hey, do you know you have, like, blue stuff all over you?"

He snickered and walked off. I checked myself in a mirror. He was right. I had giant dark-blue blotches all over myself. Talk about turning red (on top of the blue).

But believe it or not, worse things can happen.

1

Things so horrible, so gross, so incredibly mortifying that you swear you'll never tell a soul. And yet some of you did spill it all . . . in this book.

Some brave kids out there decided to share their most embarrassing moments with all of you. They talked, they wrote, they e-mailed. These are *their* stories, told in their very own words.

They came from all over the United States and from England, too. (Yes, we changed their names — after all, we are not totally cruel. But they know who they are.)

We also interviewed some wise souls who shared their Words of Wisdom (WOW) on how to deal with it all.

As you read these tales of total humiliation, just remember: They could have happened to you. Because there comes a time when each and every one of us wants to whisper, *"Tell me this isn't happening."*

The good news is that everyone gets a turn in the embarrassment spotlight. The bad news is that it still happens no matter how old, rich, or famous you get.

That ink story is pretty bad. But my best friend's story is even worse. She was sitting in the front of the class — this is an important detail —

when she fell asleep. (It was algebra, so maybe you can sympathize.) That wasn't so bad, except she started to snore. Loudly. Our math teacher was lecturing and standing up in front as usual. He was only a few feet away from her. So he strolled over to the desk where she sat, head drooped to one side, mouth open. He tapped her shoulder. She continued to snore.

He tapped her again. She woke up with a jerk, and the whole class cracked up.

But even she should feel better once she reads what's happened to the people in this book. Much better.

Chapter One

Sports-o-Trauma

Participating in sports is good for our self-esteem, or so we're told. Well, this is true — most of the time. Sometimes we're totally awesome jocks. But sometimes it feels like we're — er — more like awesome jokes.

Making Waves

One summer day in the middle of July, I went to the pool in the city. I climbed up on the high diving board and jumped in. When I came up, I noticed something was wrong. Something was missing.

The top to my bathing suit was off. I tried to put it back on under the water, but the lifeguard thought I was drowning and couldn't come up —

so he jumped in the water and pulled me out! I still wasn't wearing my top. And he held me up in front of everybody! I was so embarrassed. Everyone laughed.

I learned a lot about bathing suits. Never, never, I mean never, wear an oversized swimsuit. If you do, clip the suit or at least hold it up whenever you're in the water. You never know. What happened to me could happen to you.

— Tasha

Touchdown

When my friends asked me to play football with them one day, I definitely said yes. I loved playing football and this time I'd be playing with all girls and no boys. I jumped at the chance, thinking that it would be a lot of fun. But, after this experience, I thought I'd never in my whole life play football again.

It all happened about two weeks ago, on my birthday. It was Friday the Thirteenth, so something was bound to happen. I was playing football with my friends — Deedee, Kyla, Madelaine, Jody, and Sienna — on the school playground behind the basketball court. It was lunchtime and we had just finished eating. It was an excellent day for the game. The sky was blue; it wasn't too cold or too hot, and the sun was shining beautifully.

Not only was the weather great, the game started out great, too.

After we played for fifteen or twenty minutes, the score was tied. And my team had the ball. It was the last chance we had to win the game. Madelaine had the ball and threw it to me at the sixty-five yard line. Everyone was counting on me to make the last touchdown to win.

But I was so nervous that I started running the wrong way with the football! When I got to the one hundred yard line, thinking that I made the last touchdown and my team had won, Cheyenne, from the other team, shouted that I had scored for her team! I was so embarrassed that I felt like running all the way to Mexico!

The other team had won and it was all because of me. Everyone who was watching was laughing.

Now, every time I play, the people on my team always tell me which way to run, in case I forget. I laugh about it every time I think about it. It's hilarious *now*. But it wasn't at the time.

— Chris

Exhibition

I take private tennis lessons with a couple of other girls and my sister. We were playing a game in which you had to run to one side of the court, touch the dividing curtain, and run back to the net without another person tagging you.

I was running to get to the net and instead of stopping and turning right back around, I decided to keep running so I wouldn't lose my speed. I'd just put my hand out to the side to touch the net, but I tripped over it instead. I fell to the cement court and skinned my knees. They started bleeding. That was bad enough.

But, I was also wearing one of those short tennis skirts. It came flying up right in front of everybody, including my male instructor!

He and my sister were cracking up. At least the other two girls weren't laughing. I think they realized I was hurt.

— Kara

Slider

One Tuesday night, before dinner, my dad and I went out in the front yard to play catch.

The first ball Dad threw was a grounder. The second ball was chest-high.

And with the third ball, Dad said, "Jeanie, you had better get farther back, because this is going to be high!"

I moved back and Dad threw the ball. I jumped in the air and caught the ball, but I landed face-first in the mud. People in cars were looking at me from the street and my dad was laughing.

— Jeanie

Score?

Last winter, I played on a basketball team. We were really good, and we made it to the play-offs for the third time in a row. But by the time our game was over, the fans were yelling and laughing at me.

It was the first round of the play-offs. I played for the Tigers — the other team was called the Spartans.

The game started, and it was good. We were switching off baskets. The score was tied up most of the game, but I made twenty points.

There were ten seconds left. We were down by a shot. I was so happy when I got the ball. But I shot it at the wrong basket! I lost the game for my team. I was really embarrassed and felt really down. I just hope we can make it to the play-offs again next year.

— Mac

First Down

Once I went to football training on a Saturday. I was eight, and sometimes I didn't know if my football boots were fastened. We were playing a football match, and I was going to score. But then my lace came undone, and I didn't.

That wasn't all. In front of me was a pile of mud and a stone. I was standing on the stone. But somebody kicked it, and I went flying into the mud!

Everybody was chuckling at me, even the referee.

— Asher
(from England)

Chillin'

When I was five, a letter came in the mail. It was about skating lessons, and I got all excited because I wanted to learn to skate. My mom looked at me like she was going to say no, but after a bit of begging, she said yes!

We had to wait until the machine that smooths the ice was off the rink. As soon as I got on the ice I fell. I started to go but didn't know how to stop and I slammed into the boards. When I started to skate again, I finally managed to stop. I was so excited that I was jumping up and down. Everyone was looking at me like I was stupid.

When I got off the ice, my mom took off my skates. There were blisters all over my feet. They looked like stew bubbling up. But now, after seven years of skating, I am a hockey player for a city team.

— Aaron

One-Two-Three

My most embarrassing moment was when I had to do a dance in front of the whole school. I got into my position and started to line dance. It was fun. When I was done, though, I fell off the stage!

— Mindy

Sour Notes

One year in baseball, my team made it to the championships. We thought it was cool to be one of the best teams in baseball — until the day of the game.

The mother of a friend who was on the team made a bell for each of us with our name on it. Our moms took the bells to ring whenever we came up to bat throughout the championship game. I was embarrassed before the game even started!

— Joshua

Head over Heels

My most embarrassing moment was when I was in gym class. It was my turn to do a cartwheel and when I went up, I didn't know how to do one.

I was too shy to ask. I just reminded myself how everyone else had done it. I ended up making myself roll instead of doing a real cartwheel! Everyone laughed at me.

I'm nine and a half and I still don't know how to do a cartwheel.

— Trey

Words of Wisdom:
Some Experts Offer a Little Advice on Handling Embarrassing Situations

At the end of each chapter, look for more "Words of Wisdom." These guys really know what they're talking about.

Alvin Gentry, Detroit Pistons' head coach

We all embarrass ourselves at some point. Don't get down about what happened. Just remember, even the coolest people embarrass themselves, too. Would you believe even Michael

Jordan has shot an air ball from the free throw line? Yes, it's true. The greatest people do embarrassing things sometimes.

His Own Embarrassing Story

I was a kid in the seventh grade and had to give an oral report about a European country to my class. I was nervous as could be, having to speak in front of so many people. Just as I was starting the report, I pulled a map down from above the chalkboard to show everyone my country. I pulled the map and the whole thing went straight down to the floor. The class erupted in laughter and my train of thought was ruined.

The laughter actually calmed me down, though, and got me through the report. Because everything went from being so serious to being more funny, I was less nervous and able to give my report much more easily than I would have otherwise.

Kevin J. Anderson, _X-Files_ and _Star Wars_ novelist

The thing you need to get clear in your mind is, _What do I care what other people think?_ All through life, people are going to be laughing at you for one reason or another — it happens to everybody, because none of us is perfect. We all make mistakes.

People used to laugh at me because I wanted to be a writer. I read books all of the time, and I actually studied at school. Now, I'm an internationally best-selling author.

It's okay to be embarrassed, and it's not the worst thing in the world. Realize that every one of those people laughing at you has done something just as stupid in their lives . . . or maybe even something stupider.

I was a nerd in school, a skinny kid with glasses. I was always the last to get picked for the sports team, etc. After a while, I realized that what really mattered was what I wanted to do. I set my goals and focused my efforts — and I made my dreams come true.

John Herrington, head coach of Harrison Hawks, Michigan high school football championship winner for several years

I would tell [whoever's goofed up in a major way] that I probably made a mistake much like his or hers when I was young, and though I was embarrassed at the time, I now look back at it as a funny time, not an embarrassing one. If someone laughs, just remember, they are laughing at the situation, but not really at you. Accept that and laugh with them.

Chapter Two

Friends and Other Dangerous Creatures

Amazingly enough, it's often the people we hang with (our buds) and people we live with (our family) who get us into the most horribly embarrassing situations. We end up looking totally foolish, while they stand around laughing, or worse!

They love us, they torture us. And no matter how geeky we think we look, we can always count on them to make us look even geekier.

Pucker Up

I was six years old and lived in my old house. I was watching television when my sister, a nine-year-old, told me to kiss the floor. If I didn't do it, she was going to tell everyone at my school that I had a girlfriend.

So I told my sister, "Well, just once, okay?"

When I got done kissing the floor, I went to wash my lips, but then I noticed that my mom had videotaped the whole thing!

— Sean

Fright Night

This Halloween, the houses in my neighborhood looked really scary. I was trick-or-treating with my friends Cisco and Kerry, and I was getting scared because they kept popping out at me. Then they hid behind a bush near a really creepy-looking house. While I was waiting, they came out screaming. They were afraid of the house, too.

The house had dead flowers in the garden, the door was slanted, and there were big lumps in the ground that looked like people had been buried alive there. It looked like the Addams Family's house. I really didn't know if it was real or fake. My friends made me go up to the door first.

I rang the doorbell and a guy came out with a

Michael Myers mask on and a fake ax with blood on it! I ran down the street screaming.

— Carl

Floor Show

I was at my grandmother's house. It was the day after Christmas. I was trying to show my sister how I could slide up and down the hallway in my socks. I was trying to make this move and to look cool. I was saying, "Look at me. I bet you can't do this." I didn't see there was water on the floor. I started running and then I fell down on my butt.

— Phoebe

All Fall Down

One day, I went to dance class and enjoyed it. But it took me a while to get dressed afterward. After I was finished, my mom picked me up. Then she and I went to a jewelry store. When I got out of the car, the most embarrassing thing happened. My ladybug underpants fell out of my overalls! I was so embarrassed that I ran back to the car with my mouth wide open.

My mom and two other people, named Gina and Rhett, saw it. Then, when we went into the store, my mom told Dennis, the owner of the store, what had happened.

Finally, when I got to the back of the store I saw a Beanie Baby that I wanted, and my mom bought it for me. My mom said it was for making her laugh.

— LaTonya

Brotherly Love

"Yes, it's my big day today, Bro," I announced.

"Why?" he asked.

"I've got a date."

"Lucky you," he said. "Where are you going?"

"I'm going to see *Speed Two*," I answered.

"I don't see Mum giving you the money for that."

"I'm paying for it out of my bank account," I said.

Then my date arrived. She had thick blonde hair, and she was wearing a skirt. I was in the shower at the time. My date asked where the bathroom was. My brother told her it was straight up the stairs and through the door in the front. My date walked up the stairs and opened the door!

"Arrr!" I shouted as I jumped out of the shower and ran into my bedroom to get changed.

The date went well, but I'm never inviting a girl to my house again!

— Greg
(from England)

Olé!

My most embarrassing moment was when my mom took my family and me to her restaurant. The music was turned up very loud and the place was packed. My mom pulled me in as if I were a flipper on an arcade machine. The next thing I knew I was in front of the crowd!

My family went on to get a table. "Thanks a lot," I said.

My mom was wearing black boots and a shiny

black zippered shirt. I was wearing overalls, a light-blue shirt, and brown climbing shoes.

Suddenly, my mom put on a sombrero. Then she put one on me, too! Then she started swinging me in the air. We did a Hispanic dance, with tapping, kicking, and all of that other stuff.

Everyone took pictures, and then it was finally over. I was so relieved!

— Colleen

With Friends Like These

My brother rode his bike to the woods, and I thought that I should follow him. But my friend Giles had other ideas. First Giles squirted me with his water pistol, then my pants fell down. Everyone saw me! Giles took off, and then I ran away, too. But I forgot to pull my pants up, and they'd fallen completely off. So Giles grabbed my pants and threw them on the roof.

— Frank
(from England)

When I woke up I asked my mom, "Are you going to my game or to the churchwide craft fair?"

My mom said, "Both."

"Yippee!"

I went to get my baseball uniform on, and we left for the church at seven-thirty A.M. We got to the church at seven-forty-five. Nothing embarrassing happened there. But then it was time for the game, which was at Macalay Park. My mom sat in a lawn chair on the sidelines, cheering for our team.

I was third up at bat. The first two kids had gotten out by pop-ups.

The pitcher threw a curveball. I hit it! Everybody started to laugh. I didn't know why, so I kept running.

Then I looked at my mom. She had fallen through the lawn chair and her pink panties were showing! Everyone was trying to help her, but they were laughing so hard they couldn't pick her up. She was tangled in the lawn chair. Finally, one man was able to get her out of the chair. She was hurt a little, but at the time I was only thinking

23

about myself. I have never been so embarrassed in my life.

At third base, all of my teammates were laughing and pointing at me. I just kept my face down. The next batter hit a home run. I ran home and scored a point. Then I had to go back to the dugout. I really wanted to go home.

As I was walking to the dugout, the coach said, "Way to go, Ronald."

My teammates were still laughing. I just turned to them and said, "That's not my mom!"

— Ronald

A Nose for Trouble

One bright and sunny day, I was with my baby-sitter, Janice, and my annoying sister. I got some chips and cold root beer.

We drove around the city. My sister and I started to sing songs, but we got tired of singing. Soon Janice turned on the radio. (After all, you can't drive without music, can you?)

My sister and I started to eat and drink in the car. I put some chips in my mouth and drank some ice-cold root beer to wash them down. Right then, my sister told me something way too funny. I started to laugh so hard that root beer came out of my nose!

— Consuela

Trippin'

It all started at two-thirty when my teacher said we had fifteen minutes to finish our work. Soon I was done. Then five minutes later the class was, too. My teacher said, "Go to your lockers."

So I walked outside and my friend said, "Your shoes are untied."

I didn't believe her because she always told stories. So I didn't realize that my shoestrings had gotten caught under one of my shoes. And my buckle had gotten caught onto the strings. All of a sudden, in front of a lot of people, I started walking funny and wobbling. Everyone started laughing.

I just said, "So what?"

And then I fell. Everyone started laughing harder. I wanted to cry but instead I laughed along with them. Then I ran to my friends, pretending I had done that on purpose.

— Lorelei

Romeo and Juliet

We went into the hall to practice the Christmas concert and it was fine. Mira was talking to Amber. Mrs. Boker asked, "What are you talking to Amber about?"

She said, "I'm telling her that I don't love Zack Littlehouse anymore."

My hands went to my head, then I looked at the floor. Some people were laughing at me. I felt embarrassed.

Then I said to Mira, "I never loved you, either."

We walked to class.

— Zack
(from England)

Sticky Situation

At the beginning of the year, my friend decided to buy one of the caramel apples my school was selling. She got it about the end of lunch, so she didn't have enough time to eat it all. I helped her out a little. I ate so fast that I didn't realize that I got sticky caramel stuck to my nose, chin, and lips.

As I was walking to my locker, I passed my crush. He looked at me strangely. I asked my friend if I had anything on my face.

She said, "No, nothing at all."

I believed her. But guess what? By the time I got to my next class, about everyone I passed had seen me looking like a "caramel girl."

— Lea

We All Scream for Ice Cream

I loved my dog. When I was really young, I let him eat my ice cream with me in public. One day, I was walking around with my mom and my dog. My mom did not know I was sharing my ice cream with the dog, but then she found out. I got in trouble, and she threw the ice cream away.

She bought me another one and I shared that with my dog, even though I knew I wasn't supposed to. My mother had told me to share and I did.

Then she asked for a bite of my ice cream, and I gave her one. I said, "Mama, you eat after Doggy." She spat the ice cream out. Everybody was looking at my mom. It was funny but embarrassing.

— Tuesday

Bull's-eye

My family was having a barbecue and a birthday party for my cousin's first birthday. My auntie had made delicious food. The cake was a Barney cake. Everyone was enjoying themselves and eating at the same time.

My cousin ran up to me and gave me a hug and a kiss. I handed him his present. Then he and I started dancing. Finally, I picked him up and noticed he was wet. So I asked his mother where his diapers were. I found them, I got his wipes, and I sat him on the bed.

Before I knew it, he'd peed on my face! I rubbed my face with his wipes, and stayed in the house until the party was over.

— Zoe

Words of Wisdom

Amanda Bynes, who plays Ashley on Nickelodeon's <u>All That</u>*

My advice would be — don't feel really embarrassed but laugh at yourself instead. If you trip in front of a group of people, make a joke about how clumsy you are.

Her Own Embarrassing Story

During my first session on *All That*, Kenan Thompson and I were doing a scene together where we were playing Ping-Pong. During the scene, we hit our heads together by accident and I hit my mouth with the Ping-Pong paddle. When I looked down at my hand, I was holding a big puddle of blood. I was so shocked that I started screaming bloody murder. Everyone on the set came rushing over to make sure I was okay. That was pretty embarrassing.

Even though I was embarrassed, I really had gotten hurt so nobody laughed.

If something embarrassing happens to you, it's not the end of the world. Nobody's perfect.

Elizabeth Punsalan, World Championship ice dancer/skater and Jerod Swallow's skating partner

My advice to someone who has just done something very embarrassing would be to make light of the situation. Picture how funny it would be if it weren't happening to you. Think of how funny it will be later when you can retell the story to your family and friends.

Realize that people aren't laughing at you, they're laughing with you — even though it doesn't feel good at the time. If you're a good sport about it, they will realize what a strong character you have.

Her Own Embarrassing Story

When I was a junior skater, we (my former partner and I) were skating in a gala exhibition of champions in Germany. We had already performed and were required to do one final trick and then take a bow. My partner lifted me and we glided across the ice, and then we crashed into the boards headfirst, and tangled into a pile on the ice! The people in the front all stood up and looked over the boards to see if we were okay. But our skating friends were lined up on the ice, having a good laugh at our expense. We laughed it off, but I was horrified at the time.

Ray Roberts, tackle, Detroit Lions

If everyone is laughing, you shouldn't get upset. Instead, join in and by doing so, the laughing will make the moment less embarrassing.

His Own Embarrassing Story

When I was in the fourth grade, I had to write

something on the blackboard and when I was writing, I dropped the chalk. I bent over to pick it up and that's when I split my pants.

I was so embarrassed at first but then I started laughing because the sound that my pants made was so loud.

Chapter Three

That's "Clothes" Enough

We all want to look good. That's why we read fashion magazines, check out what the celebrities are wearing on TV, even watch *House of Style*. And yet, sometimes, it feels like wicked little gremlins are living in our clothes, planning our next major embarrassment.

Just when you think you're at your super-cool, stylin' best is when disaster is most likely to happen.

Fashion Crashin'

I hadn't seen my second-oldest sister, Leanne, in a long time. We talked, went shopping, and went to a movie. She told me all about the fashion show she was going to be in. It would raise money for the homeless. And then she asked me if I would like to be in it, too! I jumped at the chance.

When we got to the fashion show, we had our hair and our makeup done. Everything was going fine. People were taking pictures of me. I felt like a superstar. But when I was walking down the runway, I tripped! My heel got stuck between the rug and the floor, and I fell right on my butt. Some people laughed at me, and I wanted to cry out loud.

I got back up and ran backstage. I ran to the bathroom stall and cried. I'd never been so embarrassed in my whole life. I told myself I would never model or wear heels again.

My sister came into the bathroom and told me that she had done the same thing, but I know she was just saying that to make me feel better.

— Monique

Wedding Daze

One day, Mom announced, "Joshua, you are going to be a ring bearer in a wedding."

"Really, I am?" I said in a sarcastic way.

"Really," she said. "And we're going to the rehearsal today."

So we drove in silence to the town where the rehearsal was being held.

After practicing, Angie (who was getting married) gave presents to everyone who was in the ceremony. Finally it was the big day. Everyone else had gone out. I stepped into the aisle. Then I heard laughing all around me.

I looked down and ran off screaming, because my pants had fallen down!

— Joshua

Man's Best Friend?

My most embarrassing moment was at a dance. When my mom came to pick me up, she had brought my dog. We left the dance, my dog jumped on me, and I fell into an enormous mud puddle. When I got up, I was soaked in mud. Everyone saw me and started laughing. It was not at all funny to me. I messed up my shoes and clothes. I looked a lot like the Swamp Thing!

If you were me, you'd put a huge paper bag over your head and would not show your face ever again. It was the most horrible thing that could happen to a girl trying to make a fashion statement. I wanted to scream at my dog for doing what he did. It just goes to show you that you ought to train your pooch.

— Maria

Pinky

One Friday morning, my friend Camille called and asked if I could come over. My mom said yes! I told Camille I'd be over in about thirty minutes. I wanted to pick my own outfit, but my mom made me wear stretchy pink leggings and my white, pink, purple, and blue bunny shirt. I almost didn't want to go. Then we drove to Camille's house.

We were playing in Camille's mom's bathroom when Camille said I had a hole in the back of my pants. I looked in the mirror and, sure enough, there was a hole right smack in my pants — the worst thing is that it was on my butt.

We were playing in the living room when the doorbell rang. It was my mom. She and Camille's mom started talking about all kinds of stuff. I told my mom that I wanted to go, but she kept talking. Finally we were leaving, but it was too late.

Camille's older brother, Tim, came out of his room and yelled, "You have a hole in your pants!"

I told my mom I wanted to leave, and we did. When we got home, I ran to my room and changed into my jeans. I went into the living room and started tearing up the pink leggings. I told my mom that I never wanted another pair of leggings again, especially pink ones.

— Finola

Hanging Around

I was at the playground playing with some friends after school. At one end of the playground, an elderly woman was pushing a baby on a swing. Between them and me was an oak tree. That's where my story begins.

My friends and I were playing a game of shark tag. I was it. Then Jeb bet that if he climbed to the top of the oak tree I couldn't tag him. I bet him five dollars that I could. I started climbing up after him and all was going well until I was three-quarters of the way up. That's where I slipped, fell about two feet straight down, and landed on a branch.

I decided to give up on the bet, which was bad enough. I started climbing down. Then I slipped again. On my way down, a large branch caught on my pants and made a two-inch rip. I had to take my sweatshirt off and wrap it around my waist so that it would cover it. Unfortunately, my friends and the old woman caught a glimpse of the torn pants anyway. As I was leaving the playground, my friends were practically laughing their heads off.

It was especially hard to walk home while trying to cover the tear in my pants. However, I learned something from this whole experience. Never carry out bets!

— Ryan

Get a Grip

As I tried on my new dancing dress, the strap was a little bit loose and came down — in front of all my family. I was so embarrassed that I ran off with the strap still hanging down.

Downstairs, all you could hear was laughing. I was so upset that I never wanted to see them again.

Then, before everyone went home, they all wanted to come and say good-bye.

But I had an idea. I would get my chair and block the door. After a short time, the door started to open. I didn't know what to do. I started to think, *Let's make up*. The day ended with a big hug and a change into a normal top.

— Jane
(from England)

Swing Out, Sister

It all started on my first day of third grade. My mom made me wear pigtails with pink bows and a pink Tinkerbell dress with lacy sleeves. And the worst thing about it was my pink underwear.

Our class went out for recess and my friend and I ran right for the swings. I got on and started swinging, and all of a sudden a gust of wind blew my dress right over my face and showed my bright pink underwear! I screamed, "Arrrghh!"

I pulled my dress down as fast as I could. Then, my teacher, Mrs. Morton, blew the line-up whistle. But needless to say, the rest of the day my face was as red as my hair, and that's pretty red!

— Lucy

Dr. Anne Beal, columnist for *Essence* magazine

First, keep a sense of humor about things. Because even at your worst moment, rather than laughing *at* you, the class will be laughing *with* you.

Her Own Embarrassing Story

Once I was hanging out with a bunch of friends, walking to the store. It was raining and I was singing "Singin' in the Rain" and skipping through the puddles. Just like in the movie, I was deliberately stomping into the muddy water. Right at the moment when I was really trying to splash my friends, I kicked out my feet and fell right into the puddle! They laughed. I laughed.

If people are being mean and not laughing with you, they're really not your friends.

With my friends, we've decided we can't be

embarrassed about anything. We're not trying to be cool or put on airs. We're being ourselves.

When other people experience embarrassing moments and you laugh, you eventually forget all about it. Realize people approach you in the same way. They may laugh, but they also forget about it quickly.

Kevin Weekes, goalie, Vipers, Detroit hockey team

His Own Embarrassing Story

It was a play-off game, a best-of-seven series, and my team was down three games to one. I let in a goal from the other end of the ice, right through my legs. I couldn't believe it! I just counted to five and told myself that I wasn't going to let any more goals in and I didn't. We ended up winning the game and the series as well.

When you get embarrassed, you should communicate with people who are important to you, like your parents. They can give you positive feedback so that you don't get so down on yourself. Don't let these moments affect how you feel about yourself. They happen to everyone.

Chapter Four

Bathroom Bloopers

Sometimes, we call these places "rest rooms." However, as you'll soon see, they often turn out not to be all that restful. Instead, they seem to be magnets for mishaps.

Excuse Me!

I was at a movie theater with my friends when we decided to go to the bathroom. Usually, the girls' bathroom is to the left, so we went to the left side. My one friend fixed her makeup in the mirror. Suddenly, a boy came out of the stall and looked at us. He said, "Are you boys or something?"

My friend stuttered something that I couldn't

hear. I was too embarrassed. The rest of us said, "We have to go," and ran out of there.

The worst part was that boy was at the same movie with us!

— Sharinna

Stuck on You

This happened when I was three years old. I had to go to the bathroom. And when I sat down, I fell in! My butt got soaked. I could not get out no matter how much I tried. I started yelling for help. The more I worked to get myself out, the more stuck I was. I kept screaming for my mom and finally she came. She had to pull me out. I felt so silly.

— Felicia

Oh, No

One day I was in a hurry. I had to go to the bathroom bad. I pulled my pants down to my ankles and sat down on the toilet seat. Unfortunately, I forgot to lock the bathroom door. Sure enough, in walked my older brother!

How embarrassing. He teases me about it to this day.

— Melynda

Gotcha!

In the summer, my cousins came to sleep over.

My cousin C.J. said, "Let's play board games." So first we played Monopoly.

But my other cousin wanted to play hide-and-seek in the dark. My uncle came over just as we started to play.

When I went to hide, my cousin found me fast. So I had to be It for the first time. I was frightened, because it was dark and Robin always jumps out and scares the person who is It.

I found my sister trying to dig down under the clothes in the closet. "I got you," I said, but I couldn't reach her. I dug in some more and said, "I found you!" She started laughing, so I said I was going to the bathroom to look around for more people.

Just as I said "I got you," I heard my uncle say

44

he was going to the bathroom. But I hadn't put two and two together. I was already in the bathroom when he arrived, and I didn't know what to do. I was scared so I jumped into the bathtub, where I found my cousin hiding.

My uncle heard C.J. laughing so he opened the glass and plastic thing on the bathtub and found us. We were laughing, so he started laughing, too.

— Cassie

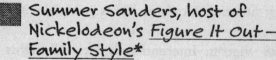

Words of Wisdom

Summer Sanders, host of Nickelodeon's Figure It Out — Family Style*

You have to laugh when something embarrassing happens. It's usually better if a friend is with you, so they can laugh with you.

There are two ways you can look at the situation: They're either laughing at you or laughing with you. Always interpret it as them laughing with you and then laugh yourself. They'll be caught off guard and you'll look confident.

Her Own Embarrassing Story

In seventh grade, I was a cheerleader, and one time we were having a contest in front of the whole school. The seventh- and eighth-grade cheerleaders were leading the classes in chants to see who would scream the loudest. The eighth graders went first and when my group got up to lead the seventh graders, I spaced out and started screaming the eighth-grade chant — instead of my own — at the top of my lungs. The whole squad and the whole school stopped their chant and just stared at me.

I just said, "Oh, well," laughed, and moved on. I didn't make a big deal out of it.

Every situation is only as big as you make it.

Karen Lee, spokeswoman for Elite, Elite Model Management Corporation/John Casablancas

On coping with an embarrassing moment, I recommend two things — acceptance and laughter. We've had models trip or fall while doing a show. . . . They just pick themselves up and continue with confidence!

Chapter Five

Party Poopers

We all loooove parties, but let's face it, they can either rock or reek. Or both. Anything can happen when you get a bunch of people together who are all trying to have an excellent time. Anything can happen. Just remember that.

Teeth on the Loose

The most embarrassing moment of my life was when my gran came to my birthday party and she had forgotten to put her denture cream on her false teeth. She put music on and started to dance. As she was dancing, her teeth flew out onto the floor! All of my friends laughed, and my gran quickly picked them up and put them back in her mouth.

— Matthew
(from England)

The Big Trip

I was going to my grandma's for her birthday. I got all dressed up in my white trousers and some really high sandals. When we got there, my aunty, my uncle, my cousins, and I played hide-and-seek about eight times. I even played the piano a little.

Grandma gave us some money and we ran over to the store, but I didn't get far, because I tripped and got mud all over my white trousers. I went back and Mum cleaned them up a bit, but I still had to go around with muck all over one leg all day.

— Treena
(from England)

Minnie the Menace

It was my ninth birthday and my best friend was coming over to spend the night. Irene came over and we gossiped, played, and drew pictures. When my sister came home, I told her what she had been missing out on.

That night I opened my birthday presents. The best gifts were from my grandparents. They'd brought three nightgowns with Minnie Mouse on them, showing many expressions like happiness, sadness, anger, surprise, fear, and curiosity. The nightgowns had my name, my sister's name, and Irene's name on their sleeves. My grandma said they'd brought the camcorder to tape us acting out the six moods of Minnie.

I put on my nightgown and Irene did my hair. We were ready for our show. As we walked out, Granddad turned on the camcorder. First we showed happiness, then sadness, then curiosity, then surprise, and then anger. That's when it happened. I was walking backward when I fell over our box of figurines! Everyone started laughing except my best friend Irene.

— Madeline

For Me?

It was my birthday and I had just turned nine. My mother's friend Clarissa came over with a present for me. I flopped on the chair and shook it. It felt like clothes, all soft and smooth. But when I opened it, I nearly burst into tears.

I ran upstairs and hid my head in my pillow. My mom came running up the stairs and said, "It's not so bad. We'll take it back, won't we?"

"Yes!" I said.

Clarissa went home and everybody came in to my room. Shall I tell you what the present was? It was a bra. I was not that old!

— Theresa
(from England)

The Right Moves

One summer, my brother and I had a party together. My brother had invited the cutest boys. I had invited the best-looking girls. Everyone wore bell-bottoms. Mine were a little too big, but I didn't care.

Then the party began. We played hide-and-seek and tag. We also did the limbo. I thought to myself, *This is going to be the best party ever.*

Then it was time for the Macarena. The boys sat on the grass. Two brave girls and I went up to dance. Everyone was looking at me.

Then all of a sudden, everyone was laughing. I

had no idea why. Until I realized what had happened. My pants had fallen down. Tears came into my eyes and I ran into my house.

This party was the worst! I put on pants that fit me and went outside. My brother sang, "Neva's pants are falling down, falling down, falling down. . . ."

I stuffed cake in his face. So I was the one with the last laugh!

— Neva

So Smooth

My best friend had her birthday party at a popular roller-skating rink. A lot of kids from the school were there. We were all having an awesome time. Soon they called all of the guests at the party over for pizza. "Everyone from party number fifteen come to your table." I was extremely hungry so I skated over to our table. I started skating slowly. But a bunch of people were skating extremely fast behind me.

So I had to go faster or I would get run over. I sped up. I was coming to a sharp turn and I did a nice-looking crossover. But before I knew it, I fell flat on my face! I was so embarrassed. I was thinking, *Tell me this isn't happening!*

Well, to tell you the truth, everybody laughed. Especially some of the boys. I didn't even know some of them. By the next day, most people had stopped making fun of me. Now I think it was hilarious and I am able to laugh about it. But at the time I was totally devastated.

— Selena

Words of Wisdom

Jason Hanson, kicker, Detroit Lions

Don't get too down on yourself and remember that embarrassing things happen to everyone.

Laugh and try to move on by having as much fun as you can.

Erin Dean, who plays Robbie Stevenson, on Nickelodeon's The Journey of Allen Strange*

The most important thing in life is to find humor and happiness. If you can learn to find that in yourself, it will last you a lifetime. If someone laughs at you, don't take it to heart. Learn to admit something was embarrassing for you. Don't play it off like it didn't bother you. What was once an unbearably embarrassing moment will one day be a humorous and uplifting story for someone else.

Chapter Six

Bad Luck Marathon

Some days, no matter what you do, nothing goes right. You know how it is. You've been there. It's just one thing after another. You feel like the world is out to get you.

Sometimes these days do happen on Friday the Thirteenth, but not always. Face it, cruddy stuff can happen anytime, anywhere. You can run and hide — but bad luck will still find you.

Can't Win 'Em All
(Sometimes it's your bud who seems to be cursed)

I had a friend named Wade who loved to play basketball. In the spring, the coach told the team that there was going to be a championship game in the summer. Wade was very excited about it. He practiced a lot so he could be one of the best players. But something so embarrassing happened that you wouldn't ever want to be in his place.

For practice, Wade shot one hundred baskets in a row, every evening. Finally, that summer, the big day came. Before the tournament, the coach told the team to do their best. Wade *knew* he would do his.

The stadium filled with people and the tournament began. Wade was one of the best players, because in the previous four months he had shot so many baskets. Then, in the second quarter, it happened.

Wade caught the ball, and dribbled it down the court. He jumped up and was about to score when he felt somebody pulling him back. Wade grabbed the hoop so he wouldn't fall and hurt himself. Suddenly, he heard the crowd laughing.

Wade saw that the player from the other team had pulled his pants down!

Even worse, the hoop broke and Wade fell on his back. Fortunately, he didn't get hurt, but the game was over for that day.

There were no more games played on that

court for three weeks. It took the custodian a long time until he could replace the broken hoop.

— Tyler

P.S. Two months later, Wade's team won the tournament. Wade, the coach, and the team were very proud of themselves!

Cream with That Rug?

My friends and I get into a lot of trouble together, but Lita and I get in the most. One sunny day, Lita and I were at the school fair. It was so crowded that we couldn't move. So we left.

Lita wanted to go visit her old neighbor. Her name was Doris. We rode our bikes there. We got to Doris's, and she invited us in for some milk and cookies. But Doris wanted *coffee* for dipping her cookies. Lita and I volunteered to go half a mile away to Dunkin' Donuts to get her some coffee.

A little later, we were on our way. When we got to Dunkin' Donuts, we had sweat dripping down our faces. We went in and got Doris her coffee, then left. The first time we got the wrong kind, so we had to go all the way back to get the right coffee. Then we put the coffee in a paper bag so that it wouldn't spill and burn our hands.

When we got back, we parked our bikes in the backyard and went through the back door. All of a sudden, the bag broke and coffee went all over Doris's new lilac rug!

Lita and I froze like ice cubes.

Doris said, "Wait, I have a surprise for you."

She came back with rug shampoo and a scrub brush. Lita and I had to go there every day until the stain was practically gone. I learned never to put hot coffee in a paper bag. Lita and I still laugh whenever we think back to that moment, but I would never want to go back to that no-good, very bad day again.

— Sunny

Eye'm Not Telling

I was at my friend's house. Her mother was baby-sitting me and my baby sister. I was playing on the floor and was right under a very tall iron candleholder. I wasn't watching and fell backward onto the candleholder. One of the disklike things rolled over my face. When I got up, I screamed because I was bleeding really bad above my left eye. I had to get stitches on my left eyebrow.

I had to wear a bandage on my face for about a week or two. Right after the accident, I went to a birthday party. When I got there everyone kept asking what happened. I had to keep telling them the same thing. It was driving me crazy.

I even had to go to church like that. But that's not all. My bandage covered my eye, and I was always knocking into things. People looked at me like I was crazy. I got tired of that, too.

I hope this never happens to you. Don't ever play under an iron candleholder!

— Tobey

Nightmare Day

A long time ago, on my first day of third grade, I fell and stumbled into my teacher. She got mad and yelled at me.

That same day, I dropped my lunch onto my friend Katy. The tray cracked in half.

After recess, I went into the bathroom. I don't

know how, but I managed to let my butt fall into the water. I never knew toilet water could be so cold! My clothes were soaked.

Finally, after I thought my worst day was over, and I was finally going home, I missed my bus stop.

I had to go back to school and call my mom to come and get me. When I was getting into the car, my mom slammed my fingers in the car door. After I thought my worst day was over, it was time for bed. As I was getting into my bed, I managed to hit my head on the headboard.

I could only hope and pray that the next day would be better!

— Jade

Should Have Stayed in Bed

The most embarrassing thing happened when I went to my cousin's birthday party at her manor farm. I saw a girl who looked like Francesca from the back. So I said, "Hello, Francesca." Then I gave her the birthday present.

She turned around and I saw it was not Francesca. Then, when we got into the play area, I saw Paula lying down in the pool. I ran over to the pool slide, tripped over her, and hit my head on the slide.

I whispered, "Ouch."

Just then someone came down the slide and went right over my head.

— Kirsty
(from England)

Words of Wisdom

Greg Evans, creator of the comic strip Luann

When something embarrassing happens, we tend to take it too seriously. We *should* just laugh it off and move on, but we replay it a thousand times in our heads.

How would Luann handle it? Like any teen, she'd agonize for weeks, long after everyone else had forgotten. The best advice I can give is to think of your embarrassing incident sort of like a moth and a lightbulb — if you keep the bulb lit, the moth will keep buzzing around. Turn the light off and the moth will go away. Of course, turning off the light is the hard part. Just remember that the embarrassing incident has two lives, one in your mind and one in the minds of all the people who saw your incident. Fortunately, it dies very quickly in other people's minds. Let it die quickly in yours, too. Turn off the light.

Michelle Akers, Olympic gold medalist, champion soccer player, www.michelleakers.com

My life is filled with embarrassing moments and I am constantly being humbled by the stupid stuff I do on a daily basis. I think we need to keep our most embarrassing moments in perspective and also strive to see the gift those moments give to us and to others.

The perspective I get out of doing dumb stuff so often is that it is a huge reminder not to take life or myself too seriously. The gift, of course, is laughter and a fun and easy attitude toward life and toward our limitations and inadequacies. It's a fact. People do dumb stuff and it doesn't change as we get older, wiser, or are a world champion or not.

We all have our moments; however, the people who can laugh at themselves are the ones who are able to truly enjoy life and know the world doesn't sit on their shoulders.

Because I do dumb stuff so frequently, when the little stuff (and even medium dumb stuff) happens, I am usually quick to laugh at myself and admit I am embarrassed I could do something so stupid and have everybody under the sun witness it. Being in the public eye, I have the opportunity for this more than most. I think the trick is to not take it too personally.

Her Own Embarrassing Story

My dad and mom were divorced when I was in fourth grade. As a result, my brother and I eventually experienced both parents doing the dating thing. One time, my dad was pretty seriously dating a woman named Jean. My brother, Mike, my dad, Jean, and I all went on a day trip on the ferry to one of the islands in Puget Sound near Seattle. On the way home, we were all sitting inside at one of the booths, talking and drinking hot chocolate and coffee. As usual, Mike and I began to get on each other's nerves, and my temper ran short. After one too many remarks, I lost it and wound up trying to kick the daylights out of my brother's leg under the table.

I stared at Mike's face and swung as hard as I could and *bam*! *Ha*, I thought, *now what do you have to say to that?* But, instead of Mike screaming out, Jean's eyes went wide, her mouth fell open, and she yelled out in surprise and pain. In my anger, I had kicked Jean smack in the shin with the toe of my boot. Needless to say, my dad didn't see her much longer and I was grounded for the rest of my life.

Chapter Seven

Stressin' Under the Spotlight

Messing up is bad enough, but if you have an audience watching, it makes that face-reddening moment a zillion times more agonizing.

Why is it that we are more likely to goof up when others are around? No one knows, but it's one of those unwritten laws. The bigger the embarrassment, the bigger the crowd.

Say What?

When I was in first grade, I had a distressing experience. I was at school, and we were having show-and-tell, where kids got to share their experiences and any interesting objects. My parents and I had been to a beautiful lake and I was dying to share my experience with the class.

Some other kids went first. A girl told about her trip to the park, and a boy shared his new toy. When the teacher suddenly called, "Next?" my hand went shooting up into the air. I yelled, "Oo, oo, oo!"

The teacher finally called on me.

I didn't know much English; however, I knew Russian extremely well. (It was my home language.) Since I thought everything up in Russian, I blurted out my story about the lake in Russian. Everyone stared at me so much that I thought their eyes were going to pop out. Their mouths dropped almost two inches.

When I think about this moment, I laugh. Luckily, I know English now. I am positive the experience will not happen to me again.

— Dean

High Jump

Like everyone, I have had my embarrassing moments. But this one happened in front of everyone at school (my friends, the teacher, and my classmates).

It was Friday the Thirteenth and I knew something was bound to happen. I was on my way to art class and eager to get out of the hot, sweltering homeroom. I guess I was too eager to leave. I noticed that a small blue metal chair was pulled out. It belonged to Ian Lasker and I knew I could jump over it if I tried.

That's when it happened. As I attempted to hop over it, I tripped. I fell flat on my hands and knees, stomach-down. I thought I had flipped a full three-hundred-sixty degrees (I didn't).

According to my witnesses, I almost broke my knee. Instead I bruised it and my hand. Everyone who saw the incident asked if I was okay and needed help getting up. They all looked at me as if I were a nut or something, which made me more embarrassed than I already was. I wished I could zap myself home. And my knee hurt! I was helped to my feet.

I'm surprised to say that no one really said anything to me about this incident afterward. I especially thought the boys would taunt me about it until I was out of school. But they haven't. Yet.

— Brianna

Is Anyone There?

I played the narrator and Pinocchio in our school play. When I had done with my Pinocchio part, Donna was supposed to come on stage. But she was still getting changed. I had to repeat the line several times until she finally came on. It seemed to take an eternity for her to appear.

The whole school was laughing and it was very embarrassing. I wanted the ground to open up and swallow me, but one's wishes do not always come true. I must have walked under a thousand ladders or broken a thousand mirrors, but strangely I do not recall these events. Yet the memory of standing on that stage will haunt me till my dying day. I will never do a play again.

— Rosalind
(from England)

Wallflower

Everyone was done eating lunch, and it was time to line up for recess. On our way down the hall, my friend and I raced out of line to visit my mom, who happened to work at my school.

We peeked inside her room to say hi and to talk about how our day was going. Afterward, we tried to sneak back in line. Unfortunately, the lunch aide saw us. When we got outside, she made us both stand against this one wall of the school building that faces the playground — this is the punishment for getting in trouble during recess.

Everyone kept coming up and asking us, "Are you two on The Wall?"

They couldn't believe it, because we are normally good students. Then I started crying — and everyone saw me!

When it was time to go in, we had to tell our teachers what happened. Then my friend who also had to stand against the wall ended up blaming me.

— Jonelle

Flipping Out

One day I went to my best friend's house with two other girls to spend the night. We were trying to do cartwheels, back handsprings, and front flips. I told my best friend's dad to watch me.

I did a front flip and fell behind the couch.

When I came up, my hair was in front of my face and everybody was laughing so hard.

I said, "Very funny, people!"

My hair was also sticking up. I was so embarrassed.

— Marlena

Spelling Bee-saster

It was the day of the spelling bee at my school. I was in it. Some of the other people in it were D.J., Emily, Lila, Greg, and a girl named Kevin.

We did a few practice words, and I had to spell *milk*. That was easy. Then we went to the real round. I had to spell *purple*. I spelled it right. I was so relieved. Then it was D.J.'s turn and he had to spell *voyage*. He messed up and was out. I felt sorry for him.

After a little bit, it was my turn again. I had to spell *viewpoint*.

"V-e, oops," I said. I knew how to spell it. The audience made me so nervous I had forgotten the *i*.

I felt my face turn red. I went and sat down. I couldn't believe I forgot the *i*.

But the spelling bee went on. The girl named Kevin won.

— Alisha

Got Milk?

I went to the cafeteria with my friends. We were eating cereal for breakfast. The whole school was there. *Everyone* was there, even the teachers. I was eating while I was talking to my friends.

I heard my friend tell a joke. It was so funny that I laughed extremely hard. I was also drinking milk at the same time. Then everyone started laughing at me. I was confused. Why were they laughing at me? I realized that I had laughed so hard that milk had come out of my nose.

I felt so embarrassed. I felt bad because they all had laughed at me. I felt like my reputation was destroyed. Then I laughed at myself.

— Arnold

ABC . . . ?

My most embarrassing moment happened to me when I was in kindergarten. My class was giving a presentation on the alphabet in the school gym. Each student had one or two letters of the alphabet to say a little rhyme about. We carried a large poster with the letter and a picture on it of something that started with the letter.

I had two letters to talk about. The first was *D*, for dinosaur, and the second was *W*, for weather. I was a little nervous. When it was my turn, I walked out in front of my class and said, "*W* is for weather." Then I stopped and didn't say anything. Some of the audience started to whisper, "*D* is for dinosaur." It took a little while for me to hear what they were saying.

Then I looked at my poster and said, "*D* is for dinosaur." Everyone was smiling at me.

— Ethan

Slip-sliding Away

I was at a poetry competition and Mr. Arless, the poetry teacher, asked me to fill his cup with ice. As I was walking back from the ice machine with a cup, I tripped over someone's outstretched leg. The ice flew right out of the cup and landed on the floor with a big crash.

Everyone in the room started to laugh and point at me. I was so embarrassed that I pretended to have hurt my little finger, so that they would stop laughing. But they kept on laughing anyway, until I left the room in tears.

— Heidi

Turn Up the Volume

I had come home from my dad's on a Sunday morning to get ready for church. I put on my sunflower dress. It was short, but it was also pretty cool. My stepdad was still asleep, so my mom and I were going by ourselves.

I walked up to the front of the church to sing. In the middle of the song, I forgot the words and my voice went out. I could not believe it.

— Shauna

Have a Seat

I was part of a choir called the Angels. One day, I was at choir practice, and we were singing "Hats." When I sat down, I didn't realize my pants had slid way down. My underpants were showing. I didn't know, though, till later, since I was singing and feeling good.

My friends were laughing, though they tried not to. They felt bad for me. They told me after class what had happened. I think everyone in the room saw me.

— Anya

Words of Wisdom

Suzanne Churchman, teacher

One of the common themes I use in my classroom is that we are all human, none of us is perfect, and we always learn more from our mistakes than from our successes. Try to maintain your cool, and smile if possible. This will put those around you at ease and surprisingly enough may put you at ease, too.

If you react with anger or by running away, it leaves you open to being teased.

It was a cold, icy winter day in Kansas. The sidewalks were a river of ice. I was about eleven years old and had just begun the seventh grade a few months before. After school, my cousin (who was also my best friend) and I were walking down the sidewalk in front of school. As we approached the main street, my cousin slipped on the ice, pulling me down with her. My skirt flew up over my head. Students were everywhere and I just knew all the boys had seen how undignified I was.

Pete Ciavaglia, center, Vipers, Detroit hockey team

Embarrassing things happen to everyone. You have to realize that you are going to make mistakes. Everyone does. You have to smile and laugh at yourself. If you get so down on yourself about every embarrassing situation, you'll be in for a miserable time.

His Own Embarrassing Story

My most embarrassing moment was when I was twenty-one. I was in my first year of pro hockey, and I scored the game winner for the other team! We were tied and I was guarding a guy; he shot the puck. Our goalie stopped it, gave up the rebound, and I shot it past him!

Chapter Eight

Shopping Shockers

Stores and malls can be great places. After all, they're filled with lots of cool things like CDs, clothes, computer games, books, and food. But then there are those days you wish you'd just stayed home.

Got You Covered

This happened in Target. We were walking around the store when my brother peed in his pants. He made me stand in front of him to hide the wet spot. Everybody was asking me, "Why are you standing in front of him?"

Then we ran into one of my brother's friends. He said to my brother, "See you at the skating place."

And, since my brother couldn't think of an excuse, we had to go to the skating rink. I stood in front of him there, too. I was a little embarrassed, but I was also glad I could help out my brother.

— Heath

Red Faces — Aisle Four

My most embarrassing moment was when I was in the fourth grade. It all started on a Saturday. My family and I went to Wal-Mart to get some decorations to put around our house. We went into the store and walked through the aisles.

My shoestrings were untied and I tripped over them and fell on my hands. When I got up, my hands felt like they were on fire.

When I looked up, there were many people around and I felt embarrassed that whole day.

— Corey

Batter Up

When I was seven, I went to the supermarket. I was fooling around and dancing on the floor. My nana was laughing.

Then I started to think about baseball and Babe Ruth. I imagined that I was a big player. I grabbed a long piece of bread and pretended it was a baseball bat. I slammed it against a shopping cart. Then a lady yelled at me. I felt so embarrassed, and everyone was laughing at me.

When I was out of the store, I thought that I was going to cry. But I learned not to think about baseball at the store!

— Kiefer

Words of Wisdom

Chris Brown, creator of the comic strip <u>Hagar the Horrible</u>

Sometimes a sheepish shrug and shaking your head at your own silliness can at least tide you over until you can creep off of center stage. I think part of why kids laugh when another kid falls or spills a tray in the cafeteria is because it makes them nervous. It's the sort of thing that could just as easily happen to them — and on another day it probably will!

His Own Embarrassing Story

One day my mother bought my brother, my sister, and me tickets to see *Beatlemania* on Broadway. The day of the show my mother surprised me with a suit she had bought for me to wear on this special occasion.

She had bought the suit out of a catalog. Let me tell you about this suit. It had padded shoulders a football player would have loved. This was a bright neon lime-green polyester leisure suit and it struck terror into my heart the moment I laid eyes upon it.

We were in a taxicab driving to the theater when the skies opened up. Traffic was so heavy around the theater that the driver had to double-park in the street. When I turned around there was a wide, wide puddle of water between myself and the sidewalk.

There was no way around it — cars were parked bumper to bumper up and down the street.

And I had to get to the curb, where my siblings were beckoning to me. And now a huge truck was bearing down on me. I landed on the curb. I had completely missed the puddle. I was victorious! I had won! And then I heard the sound.

Many of you may have heard this sound before: the ripping of cloth. And you might guess that what had happened was that I had split my pants.

Brian Stablein, wide receiver, Detroit Lions

Keep your head up and try not to get down on yourself. If everyone is laughing at you, you should laugh, too, and remember that other people aren't necessarily laughing at you, instead they are laughing at the situation. It helps to find humor in the situation.

His Own Embarrassing Story

When I was in the fifth grade, I shot two air balls from the free-throw line in a game. If I had made one of the free-throw attempts, our team would have won the game.

How did I deal with it? I talked about the missing shots with my family. I also kept the mind-set that I should have as much fun as I possibly can without letting an embarrassing moment distract me.

Chapter Nine

Oops!

Mistakes happen. We misunderstand what's going on. We forget stuff. We think we know what's happening, but we're wrong. We end up feeling confused.

And sometimes people make mistakes about us. In fact, we *all* mess up at one time or another.

No Way!

Once when I was in the third grade, our class divided up into groups to do a project. Our classroom happened to be near the boys' bathroom.

One of the boys from my group came out of the bathroom and said, "Someone sneezed on the wall in there." He laughed, and then two other boys from my group went in to check it out. They came out laughing, too.

I said, "You're making it up. There isn't anything on that wall."

"Yes, there is! Yes, there is!" they shouted.

I said, "Well, then show me." I went into the bathroom and there it was! It really looked like someone had sneezed right on the wall.

When I came out, one of the boys said, "So, Evelese, we were right, huh?"

"Yes," I replied. "But what was that big, white sinklike thing in there?"

Then all I heard was a big roar of laughter.

Finally, one of the boys said, "That was the toilet!"

I had never seen a urinal (boys' toilet) before. It was very embarrassing because everyone else knew what it was.

— Evelese

Duck, Duck . . .

I can remember being really embarrassed once in my life. My dad, my grandpa, my uncle, and I were going fishing. We all went to the store to get some live bait and fishing poles. Then we went to the duck pond. There were geese and ducks in the water — they swam around a big rock. We put our chairs on the grass and tried to catch pike, sunfish, bluegill, and smallmouth bass.

I went up to the edge of the duck pond and cast my line out. My shoes started to sink in the mud. Suddenly I fell into the pond! Then, to make matters worse, a duck flew over and went to the bathroom on me!

— Lyla

Here's Toe You

I was in a gym class and my teacher told us that next week she'd pick three students from each grade to do a show. We were going to demonstrate our skills to other kids.

When the next week came, I was picked, and the teacher told me how to do toe-to-toe with a partner. I always *got* a partner, so I really didn't know that much about toe-to-toe until it was time to show the class.

We were all doing other stuff when the teacher told us to go toe-to-toe for the group that came to see us. My mind went completely blank! I looked for a partner but had no luck. And the person who was supposed to be watching was right beside me.

I panicked.

Then my gym teacher asked, "Anyone without a partner?"

I quickly jumped away and ran to the middle of the room. Everyone was already laughing. I found a person who didn't have a partner and finished the two-person drills.

— Paul

Which Is Which?

My parents, uncle, cousin, and grandparents were all at the airport. We were talking about the arrival of my grandparents in the United States when my grandfather said he had to go to the bathroom. I found a huge bathroom sign with a men's sign on the left and a women's sign on the right. I took the left.

When I saw the pink tiles on the floor, I suddenly knew something was wrong. Then a woman came up to me and said that the men's room was to the right, not to the left.

When I told my grandfather what happened, he laughed and said, "I thought you knew English!"

— Quade

April Fresh

Before she went to sleep, my mom was doing laundry and she left the basket next to my bed. The basket was full of clothes. My mom forgot all about it.

In my sleep, I was rolling and tossing on my bed. I even pulled the covers off. And somehow I fell into the laundry basket.

In the morning, at eight A.M., I heard loud laughs, and I woke up. My family had surrounded the laundry basket, because I was in it. They didn't stop laughing until they fell asleep that night. I was so embarrassed that day.

— Kira

Music to My Ears

My day was going well. At recess, I caught two touchdown passes. Then I got a hundred on my math test. That morning I had even gone to try out for the band — and made it. I told them if they needed someone to play in a concert, I was their man. Later, I practiced for ten minutes.

The next day, I was struggling to remember the rhythm of the song. The day was going awful. I found out there was a pop quiz and I hadn't studied. I thought to myself, what else could go wrong?

It was afterward that I felt so embarrassed.

We had a surprise concert, and I had to play a duet with Liam, my friend. After the fifth grade sang, it was our turn to perform.

I played fine at the beginning but then Liam messed up. He played something weird and kind of funny. Then I got confused and messed up, too. But the crowd cheered and clapped anyway. After I was done with the duet, I felt relieved.

— Reeve

For Goodness Snakes

School ended. I quickly ran out. As usual, I was eager to get home. I could play and see my pets. Sounded good. If only I knew . . .

It was Wednesday, the day I feed my snake. We drove to the pet store on the way home. I was excited about feeding my snake. I always think it is really cool. He'll eat about five guppies while I'm holding him.

When we got home, there was a boy in the driveway, and he looked about my age. I was so excited. I hardly ever have someone my age to play with. I asked my mother who he was. I thought I heard her mumble something about him being the son of my brother's tutor.

I walked over and asked if he wanted to come inside and watch me feed my snake.

He said, "I have to do those leaves."

That was when I noticed the rake and pile of leaves at his feet! He was there to do a job.

I guess I spoke too soon. I was embarrassed the rest of the day. Next time, someone else can make the visitors feel welcome.

— Moira

Too Close for Comfort

One day when I was seven, I went to the parking lot next to my house. I was trying to learn to

Rollerblade. It was a nice, sunny day and my brother and sister were helping me. I was having fun then. I knew how to turn, but not stop. So something embarrassing was bound to happen.

There was a tiny wall in the parking lot. I decided to go down a hill, but I couldn't stop. I tripped and flipped over the wall and fell into some dog doo! My brother and sister were there laughing at me. I felt so embarrassed.

When I got up to my house, I took a shower because I stunk! I have learned to go slower or to stop. Next time, I can turn away from the wall.

— Brad

Caught!

One day, a new fashion started at my school. They were called Freddies. You made them by getting rosebuds and putting two thorns at each side to make arms and two thorns at the bottom to make legs. Everybody had them except a few people.

Most kids had families of Freddies, and when the teacher was not looking, we would get them out to play with them. One day, a person told the headmaster that some people were making Freddies.

The headmaster looked at the rose plant and saw that it was a mess. Unfortunately, I was near him at the time.

He shouted, "Dameon, did you do this?"

I paused a bit and suddenly he shouted again, "Did you do it?"

I had to say yes.

— Dameon
(from England)

Words of Wisdom

Mike Prokopec, right wing, Vipers, Detroit hockey team

His Own Embarrassing Story

When I was little, I was playing in a hockey tournament in Hull, Quebec. It was a big deal because it was a big arena and was sold out. When I went to hop over the boards for shift, my teammate opened the door to come onto the bench. I

91

fell right on my head in front of everybody. I just pretended it didn't happen and went out and played.

If you don't take yourself too seriously, you can do that. Laugh it off and just go on like it never happened.

Shane Sweet, who plays Josh Stevenson on Nickelodeon's The Journey of Allen Strange*

Just realize your mistake and try to have a good sense of humor about it. Just laugh with them; nothing is worth getting mad at your friends.

His Own Embarrassing Story

I was onstage playing my guitar and my fly was unzipped. I put the guitar in front of it and zipped my fly up.

Always try to have a good sense of humor about things.

*© 1998 Viacom International Inc. All rights reserved. Nickelodeon, *The Journey of Allen*

Ron Reisler, soccer coach, Spirit of Massachusetts, statewide girls' club team, winner of divisional, regional, and state championships

It's normal to feel embarrassed, particularly if there's an audience. Realize your feelings are completely normal.

First, acknowledge how you feel. Second, don't try to blame someone else. Third, think about how you could have avoided making the mistake and try to learn from the experience. Sometimes, though, you have no control over the situation and you have to understand that. The bottom line is that you should not be too hard on yourself.

If people do laugh at you, it's partly because they are thinking they're glad that the embarrassing thing didn't happen to them. Try to laugh with them and move on. If people can't handle it or get over it, then they're not your friends anyway.

Just remember, nothing great ever happened to someone who was afraid to be wrong.

Chapter Ten

It Doesn't Get Worse Than This (Really)

There's embarrassment, and there's embarrassment. And then there's the total please-someone-tell-me-it's-a-bad-dream kind of stuff. You might want to read the following stories with one eye closed. Trust me, they are baaad. You've got to give the authors credit for their sheer gutsiness. Not many of us would dare to share such hideously humiliating tales.

Crushed

Last year, I was trying to get a guy's attention at lunch. I had liked him for about two years. I thought all was going well since he was laughing at my jokes and gestures. I left the cafeteria feeling proud of my excellent flirtatious self.

Well, it turns out that my flirting wasn't so great after all! The only reason he was laughing was that I had something gross hanging out of my nose the whole time!

— Molly

Somebody Stop Me

One day, when I was five, I went to kindergarten. I was coloring pictures when my stomach didn't feel too good. I asked the teacher if I could call my mom but she told me to go to the office. When I came back, I told her I had a fever. I got a drink of water and my hand was shaking. When I came back to the classroom, it happened.

Pop! Yuck! I'd thrown up. Was I embarrassed.

When my dad came, I felt sick again, but I thought I could hold my lunch. We were halfway to his restaurant when it happened again. *Blop.* I felt dizzy.

We got to the restaurant and I took a nap, but

that wasn't the end of the mess. *Sposh*. This time, right in front of customers! Embarrassed again.

— Terri

We Almost Didn't Print This One (because it's sooo embarrassing)

My birthday is in December, and last year it was on the last day of school before Christmas vacation. My big sister, Rose, is away at college and she was supposed to come home for Christmas vacation the next day.

We had a party at school that day. It was for Christmas and my birthday, too. We ate chocolate cake and drank punch and sang Christmas carols. We were still cleaning up the room when the final bell rang for the day. We stopped cleaning up and ran for the bus so we wouldn't miss it.

By the time we got to the first stop, I remembered that I didn't use the bathroom on the way out of the school. I had to go really bad. It was getting worse all the time, and it was still a *long* way home.

By the time we stopped to pick up some kids

from another school, I had to go so bad it hurt, but there was no time to go into their school and use the bathroom. And there were still five more stops before I would be home. I made it to the third stop, then I couldn't hold it anymore. I totally went in my pants! Everybody held their noses and got as far away from me as they could.

It seemed like it took two hours to get to my house because I was so embarrassed. Finally we got to my house and I got off the bus and walked up the driveway and went into the house. My mom is always sitting at the kitchen table drinking coffee with a glass of milk for me when I get home, and I knew I was going to have to explain to her why I had stinky pants on my tenth birthday.

But it was even worse than that! Rose had decided to surprise me and came home a day early. She came over to hug me but stopped really fast because of the smell. I said, "I have to go to the bathroom really bad." She said, "I think it's too late, but if you go in there to clean up I'll get you a clean pair of underpants out of your dresser for a birthday present."

I went into the bathroom and cleaned up, and then I went over to the door and opened it a little and said, "Rose, do you have my clean under-pants?" She handed me a package and smiled. She had gift-wrapped my underpants for me while I was in the bathroom.

It was the most embarrassing thing that ever happened to me, but I sure did appreciate her gift!

— Genevieve

A Turkey of a Day

In my life, many embarrassing things have happened to me, but the one thing I'm going to tell you about is the worst. On Thanksgiving two years ago, I was at my cousin's house and we were getting ready to eat a nice big turkey feast. I was having a jolly time with my family until the horri-ble disaster happened.

Everyone was sitting and getting ready to feast. We were all starving. My aunt brought out the turkey and we were all drooling over it.

I reached over the table because I was anxious to eat. I hadn't eaten anything all day. They all were telling me to stop and I didn't listen. Until something horrible happened. The table started to tilt and then two seconds later, the whole thing collapsed. All the food came dashing down on the floor. It splattered all over my uncle's hair and all over my aunt's new dress. The potatoes went all over my grandma's new couch.

I was so embarrassed for the next hour. Instead of having a Thanksgiving feast, we had to go to McDonald's, because everyone was broke from buying all the food for the feast.

Sometimes I can look back and laugh, but sometimes I wonder how a nine-year-old kid could ruin an entire Thanksgiving.

— Cathleen

Gotta Scratch

It was my seventh birthday, and it was time for me to cut the cake. After passing out two or three pieces, my hands were smothered in icing. Suddenly, I felt a terrible itch in my nose. I looked around to make sure nobody was watching and dug into my nose to relieve the itch.

Maybe nobody *saw* me do it. But everyone knew it, because my nose was covered in icing! To top it off, my parents caught it on tape. And to make this experience the most embarrassing of all, my parents sent the tape to *America's Funniest Home Videos* to show the world.

— Taylor

Say "Cheese"

My most embarrassing moment was when my relatives came over to visit. I had gone to the bathroom and my mom was looking for me so she could take my picture. But she didn't know I was in the bathroom. I had just finished using the bathroom and was putting on my last overall strap when suddenly Mom came in and took a picture of me!

Afterward, she waited for the picture to come out clear, and it did. She went and showed it to my relatives, and they were all laughing!

— Josefina

What a Doll

It all happened one cold Saturday night in December. I was only four years old. When my family was all asleep, I stayed up and watched *Child's*

Play. All of a sudden, Chucky's arm flew off. I began to scream. I jumped off the couch and ran into the kitchen. I began to kick and holler.

My parents stayed asleep, but my guests woke up. My uncle asked if I was okay.

"Yes!" I said.

Then they gave me a glass of water, and everyone went into the den. I saw Chucky again. This time, he had a hole in his mouth and his eyeballs were big and light, light blue. His cheeks were big and round, and his head was wide. Then he blew up and his body parts were everywhere. At the end of the movie, after the credits, they showed Chucky's head again without any eyeballs, and he smiled at me.

But I will never watch Chucky again! Ahhhhh!

— Delia

Let Me Off!

It was my birthday and I was wearing a new dress that my mom had given me, even though we were going to Cedar Point. When I got there, the first thing I wanted was a pop. I was thirsty. Then

I asked my mom if I could go on the roller coaster. She said yes. I finally got up to the front of the line and got on the roller coaster. I was a little scared, and suddenly I had to go to the bathroom really bad.

But the man said I'd have to wait until the coaster stopped. I asked the man again in a good way if I could go to the bathroom. He told me in a good way the same answer. Wait until the roller coaster stops. Then I asked him in a mean way to stop the roller coaster. So he finally stopped it. I ran and ran to the bathroom, but it was too late.

I peed in my dress and I was so embarrassed. It was a bad birthday.

— Kareena

London Britches

At school, we were getting changed for the Christmas play. I stood up to take my trousers off but my underwear came off as well! Everyone saw me half-naked!

— Brian
(from England)

Words of Wisdom

Bobby Jay, defense, Vipers, Detroit hockey team

His Own Embarrassing Story

Once when I was eleven, I rushed out onto the ice rink and forgot to take off my skate guards. I swear I was Bambi falling all over the place. I knocked over a few other players on my team. It was so embarrassing, but now I just laugh about it.

You have to be able to laugh at yourself in these instances. And if people laugh at you, you can't take it personally, it's probably funny. If you can laugh with them, they'll respect you for it.

Jerod Swallow, World Championship ice skater/ice dancer and Elizabeth Punsalan's skating partner

We all make mistakes or have embarrassing moments. We should look at them in a humorous way if possible. Find the light side of the moment and have a good chuckle at yourself. Everyone will laugh with you if you can laugh at yourself.

Remember to remind those who are laughing at you that you are only human, and humans are all very funny beings. Those people who find humor in what they do, especially if it's an embarrassing moment, are a special breed of human beings.

Chapter Eleven

You Can Open Your Eyes Now

You may be laughing to yourself right now, thrilled that none of the gross things in this book have happened to you. Or you may be feeling goofy and red-faced because one or more of these traumas *has* happened to you.

Either way, it's time to give thanks that no matter how bad the moment is, we survive. And as our Words of Wisdom guys have so aptly demonstrated, you not only will live through them, but embarrassment may make you stronger, wiser, and happier, too.

At least you know you're the member of a big club (with some pretty cool people in it).

Many of the people in this book laughed at their own disasters. You can, too — but maybe it will take a while.

But if you keep doing embarrassing stuff and you think it's really, really ultra-embarrassing and funny, why not write it down? Who knows, maybe there'll be a sequel to *Tell Me This Isn't Happening!* and just maybe you'll be in it.